John Harrison

Three Ballads

The Clipper Screw, Maximilian, Trafalgar

John Harrison

Three Ballads
The Clipper Screw, Maximilian, Trafalgar

ISBN/EAN: 9783744788038

Printed in Europe, USA, Canada, Australia, Japan

Cover: Foto ©Andreas Hilbeck / pixelio.de

More available books at **www.hansebooks.com**

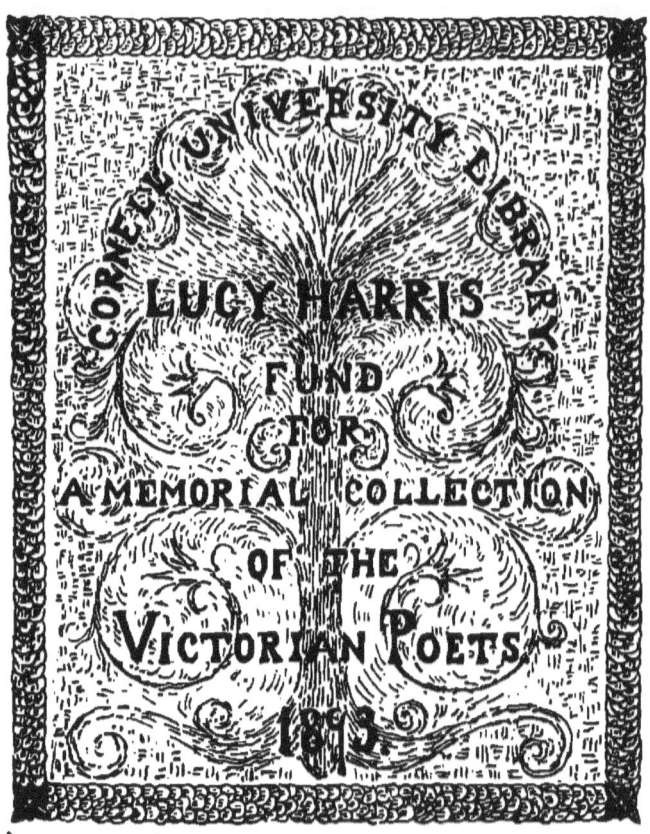

THREE BALLADS.

THREE BALLADS.

THE CLIPPER SCREW.

MAXIMILIAN.

TRAFALGAR.

BY

JOHN HARRISON.

THE PHOTOGRAPH FROM THE LIFE BY J. MORGAN.

LONDON:

LONGMANS, GREEN, READER, AND DYER.

1869.

k

BRISTOL:

I. E. CHILLCOTT, STEAM PRESS.

DEDICATED TO HIS FRIEND

MRS. REYNOLDS,

BY

J. HARRISON.

THE CLIPPER SCREW.

THE CLIPPER SCREW,

A SEAMAN'S STORY.

IN FIVE PARTS.

———◆———

PART I.

CAST off—from Ship and Mates adrift
　A broken man behold;
An Ocean waif upon the shore
　By stormy billows rolled,
He bears a message from the Deep
　That else were never told.

O thou dread Flood, whose angry waves
  Thus roughly dealt with me,
Ha'st thou no pity, no remorse,
  Thou smiling treacherous Sea?
Where are my comrades ruthless Main,
  The men who trusted thee?

Sucked in thy salt voracious maw,
  They know nor calm nor gale,
Poised fathoms down they grimly sway
  Beneath thy silvery veil,
Till one by one, they rot, are gone—
  Enough, and to my tale.

The Ship at single anchor rode
  As buoyant as a bird,
The fires were lit, the steam was up,
  Her stalwart crew aboard,
We manned the capstan bars and stood
  Awaiting for the word—

"All Hands up anchor; Heave away
  To the drums and fifes, Heave ho—
Round at the capstan bars we tramp,
  Out to the Blue we go,
Heave with a will my Hearties all
  To the drums and fifes, Heave ho,"—

"Oh who would kick his heels ashore
  To watch the grass agrowing,
For us, the billow's joyous roar
  When stormy winds are blowing.
If calm befall, 'tis just as well,
  We cheer the watch with song,
While down keel deep the ponderous screw
  Heaves the good ship along;"

"Then round with the capstan bars, my lads,
Heave to the fifes and drums,
Heave with a will, my Hearties all,
And home the anchor comes;
Heave, Boys, Heave,—Yo Ho—Heave Ho—
Heave, to the fifes and drums."

"Talk not to us of flowery vales,
Or love-sick maids at even,
Be ours the ship with swelling sails
Kissed by the breath of Heaven.
Blow high, blow low, 'tis on we go,
Yon bird is not more free,
Away, away, by night and day,
Over the stormy sea;"

"Then round with the capstan bars, my lads,
Heave to the fifes and drums,
Heave with a will, my Hearties all,
And home the anchor comes;
Heave, Boys, Heave,—Yo Ho—Heave Ho—
Heave to the fifes and drums."

The stirring chorus ceased—the ship
  Swung free upon the tide;
A signal from the parting gun—
  A farewell cheer replied,
And sweethearts, wives, with faltering steps,
  Crept down the laddered side.

Some heavy hearts had we aboard,
  And tears were shed, no doubt,
And hands were grasped in sudden heat,
  Rough hands of seamen stout;
But let that be—the wind blew free,
  The flags streamed gaily out.

The Captain spoke right cheerily,
  Though tearful many an eye;
"Good bye—clear decks—we're under way,
  God bless ye all—Good bye.
Helm hard a starboard—turn ahead,
  God bless ye all—Good bye."

Then ceased at once the sounding blast
  Of fierce escaping steam,—
The engines moved ahead—the foam
  Sluiced up as white as cream,
The Ship her starboard helm obeyed,
  Obeyed impelling steam.

The woodlands on the sloping shore
  Were rich with Autumn gold,
Though here and there the branches bare
  Of rough November told,
When we upon the lofty yards
  Did sail on sail unfold;

The shivering canvas caught the breeze;
  We cheered with three times three,
The while our Clipper smoothly cut
  Her pathway to the sea:
The brimming river, far and wide,
  Surged astern tumultuously;

We passed the Fort, the Ship on guard,
  The Lighthouse, on the right;
The kerchiefs fluttering from the pier
  They soon were lost to sight;
The waterfowl, with plaintive cries,
  Rose circling on our flight,

The parting shore-boats cheered their last,
  Dropped down the foam, were gone;
And we, across the rippled bar,
  Stood out to sea alone;
The course due south o'er half the world
  Beyond the torrid zone.

The wind upon the harp-like shrouds
  A wild farewell did play,
Brief sunshine lit the fitful sails,
  Then all was cold and grey;
The sable smoke, the furrowed foam,
  We left them on the way.

B

And now, across the widening waste
  We strained our eyes in vain,
The glimmering town, the well known cliffs,
  Soon blended with the main;
What months must pass, what leagues be run,
  Ere we come home again.

With steam and sail and ebbing tide
  We dropped old England's shore.
At noon the sky grew overcast,
  The rack drove scudding o'er,
The sea-boy high upon the mast
  Beheld the land no more;

The Ocean stretched unbroken round,
  Nor ship nor shore in sight,
The whitening waves rolled up astern,
  And urged us on our flight;
Our lofty spars against the clouds
  Swayed, circling left and right.

Before the gale we bowled along
  Four steersmen at the wheel,
With swelling sails and straining shrouds,
  And swift dividing keel,
Tossing aside the seething spray
  With swift dividing keel.

At eve, the spurt of wind died out,
  The Ship rolled to and fro ;
But where the red Sun touched the Sea,
  A squall showed white as snow ;
The Captain from the bridge sung out
  " Turn up the watch below,

"Hands, shorten sail "—for backing round,
  The wind came strong from South,
And when the Sun ,was down, the night
  Grew black as devil's mouth—
We lit our lamps, and, under steam,
  Steered right down to the South.

In two's and three's we paced the deck
  And peered into the night—
On either bow the leaping waves
  Gleamed in each signal light,
Now red, now green, now on the left,
  Now dancing on the right;

While out the funnel's iron jaws
  The swiftly issuing smoke,
Bronzed by the fiery furnace glare
  Aloft night's shadow broke—
Below, we heard the hissing steam
  And the thud of the engine stroke.

Top-gallants struck, we made all snug;
  The sea broke wild and strange,
The billows howled, low thunder growled,
  With rain and hail in change;
From South to East, and back again
  The veering wind did range,

Blustering squalls, and then a lull—
  The night, a shrouding pall,
Beyond the glimmering lights aboard
  Closed round us like a wall;
The Ship though under easy steam,
  Took seas in over all.

At midnight, when the watch was changed,
  We tumbled in below;
There, in narrow hammocks ranged,
  Swinging to and fro,
Though loud the rigging whirred aloft
  When piping squalls did blow,

Though loud the angry waves roared past.
  Keel-cloven through and through,
We, rocked asleep upon the Deep,
  Nor sound nor motion knew,
Nor dreamed that night to be our last
  Aboard the Clipper Screw.

PART II.

Dawn crept along the ocean's rim
　　Close veiled in mist and spray.
The Sun arose—we saw him not,
　　A stormdrift far away
Wound about his golden face
　　A shroud of livid grey.

From North to South, from East to West,
　　No break was in the cloud
That linking laggard Day with Night
　　O'er-arched the lurid flood:
The sails were furled—with steam alone
　　Our onward course we ploughed.

'Twas calm—our smoke for miles astern
 Lay coiled without a blast;
The sluggish waves like molten lead,
 Slow heaving, tumbled past;
The storm-forboding glass was low,
 And still was falling fast.

In restless groups we paced the deck,—
 The shadow undefined
Of coming evil fell on us
 Oppressing every mind—
The solemn cloud—the twilight strange—
 And never a breath of wind.

The Captain stood upon the Bridge,
 His spyglass at his eye ;
He swept the sea from East to West
 And silently did spy—
At last he turned, and softly said
 " God help us, by and by."

As day wore on a deeper gloom
    Obscured the quivering East,
The sea grew black as ink and still
    The monstrous gloom increased,
A fitful, gusty wind arose,
    Veered to the north, and ceased.

Far south, a ruck of snowy foam
    Lashed from the inky main,
Drove down the dark horizon's line,
    Scarce seen ere lost again
In a shrouding veil, of rain and hail,
    Of scourging hail, and rain.

We heard no sound save the creak of spars
    And the swirl of the screw alone,
Till a restless breeze 'gan stir the shrouds
    With strange unearthly moan,
And the rush of the coming storm swelled up,
    And the thunder's hollow groan;

A herald blast yelled by—and straight
  The tempest burst aboard.
The Captain shouted—in the roar
  We could not hear a word ;
He, through his speaking trumpet bawled,
  But never a word we heard.

As one, who struck by sudden blow
  Reels headlong to the plain,
The Ship heeled over, till we thought
  She ne'er could rise again ;
Her ponderous yardarms swept the foam
  That strewed the seething main,

Her huge black hull, down to the keel,
  Bared to the eye of day.
We, scrambling up the slippery deck,
  Seized bulwark, shroud, and stay,
While prone as storm-uprooted oak
  Our noble Clipper lay.

At last she righted—with a lurch
  That wrenched her iron frame
Surging from her foamy bed
  On even keel she came,
With helm hard down and labouring steam,
  Up to the wind she came.

The Boatswain shook his head, yet he
  Had roughed through many a gale;
He cast a troubled look aloft
  As he clung to the weather rail,
But the spars were hid in flying drift,
  Rain, and whitening hail.

The sea-birds, driving on the storm,
  Came tumbling fast aboard,
Blue lightning glared, but in the din
  No thunderclap was heard,
As one huge giant voice, the wind
  And raging billows roared.

The lightnings quivering on the deck
  Did sulphurous fumes exhale,
Then darting to the bowsprit end
  Were quenched in melting hail;
Shorn by the wind, the waves like dust
  Flew, blending with the gale.

The close-furled sails split out in rags;
  All Hands held hard aweather;
The blast our weighty funnel hurled
  To leeward like a feather,
Then chopped to north, and overboard
  Went masts, spars, boats, together.

Top-hamper crashing from aloft,
  Spread ruin far and wide;
The mainmast surging up end on
  Stove in the starboard side,
And through the naked ribs in rushed
  The fierce resistless tide;

Then sudden fear smote every man,
   Hearts quailed, however stout,
As the hissing waters whirled and swirled
   And the engine fires went out,
As the Ship fell off, in the hollow trough,
   And all her fires were out.

A mastless hulk, nor sail, nor steam,
   A carcase without soul,
She gave a heavy weather lurch
   And then a starboard roll—
At every lurch her brazen bell
   Rang out a single toll.

Half strangled by the driving spray
   We fought with waves and wind,
We cleared the wreck, we manned the pumps
   In companies combined,
Yet all the while we knew right well
   Our doom was sealed and signed.

Each moment deeper in the sea
  The wallowing vessel rolled,
Deep water in the engine room,
  Deep water in the hold,
The air 'tween decks rushed screaming up
  And speedy doom foretold.

'Twas strange that in this desperate strife
  For life, and life alone,
When time had narrowed to an hour,
  And Death familiar grown
Had stamped his seal on every brow,
  Our minds still held their own.

In duty steadfast, at the pumps
  Like men we laboured on;
Our breath grew shorter, yet we strove
  Till all our strength was gone,
One at my side dropped down and died—
  His last day's work was done.

We searched the drear horizon round
  But never a sail could see;
The Captain shut his telescope
  And not a word said he;
The waves leapt up like ravening wolves
  And mocked our agony.

In gangs about the rolling hulk
  We clustered here and there;
Scared Hope had fled, and Death unmasked
  Now dogged us everywhere.
Worn out,—at last we stood at bay
  And faced him in despair.

Green seas swept surging fore and aft,
  The Ship was settling fast;
A few brief words we wrote in haste,—
  When every chance had passed
The bottle with the last farewell
  Into the sea was cast.

In that dread hour, adrift, undone,
 The sport of wind and wave,
We turned to God, to Him alone
 Our hearts and souls we gave;
Then patiently we waited Death,
 Each gazing on his grave.

The end was nigh, e'en restless Fear
 Had ceased to agitate.
Huddled in silence,—on our brows
 A strange dull quiet sate,
Death's Harbinger, that kindly blunts
 The sense of instant fate.

Apart from all, his gold laced cap
 Pressed down upon his brow,
The Captain stood upon the poop
 And watched the scene below—
Decks lashed by waves, and here and there
 A corse washed to and fro.

He made no sign, gave no command,
　　His sway was ended then,—
The Chief, who scarce an hour ago
　　Had ruled three hundred men,
Had reined five hundred horses power,
　　Had ruled three hundred men.

We gathered round him—one and all,
　　A ghastly company.
His features sharp and pinched, were white
　　As foam flecks drifting by,
His lips in prayer moved, his eyes
　　Then wandered to the sky.

We prayed as he—we all looked up
　　To Heaven with faces pale.
The clouds grew lighter—the dread blast
　　Had steadied to a gale—
The thunder growled afar—the squalls
　　Had ceased of rain and hail—

The Sun shone out—in rainbow mist
  The dark storm rolled away—
The Sea still heaved in lofty waves,
  Still broke in sheeted spray,
When the Ship her mighty bows upreared
  Toward the azure day,

Then dipped the poop—the hungry flood
  Yawned wide and tumbled o'er;
In frantic haste we strove to climb
  The steep deck's sliding floor,
The tumult wild, the wilder shriek
  Were hushed for evermore

As by the stern the Ship went down
  And clove her own dark grave;
The whirlpool spinning on the top
  Broke in a foaming wave,
And still the hull slid down and down
  Into its ocean grave.

C

PART III.

Sucked in the vortex, fathoms deep
   I sank beneath the main;
Green lights were whirling in mine eyes,
   Strange phantoms in my brain,
Then came a calm ineffable,
   And then I rose again;

I rose again—grim Death with Life
   Did battle in my frame;
A twitching gasp—a sobbing breath—
   And Life, Death overcame;
I floated up a corse, and yet
   Strong Life, Death overcame;

I lived—convulsively I caught
  A hencoop, and held on;
A fluttering bird was caged therein,
  A fowl, and only one;
He thrust his head from out the bars
  While I was holding on.

No other living thing I saw,
  I heard nor shriek nor sigh;
The Ship was gone, and in her stead
  The shrouding waves rolled by;
There was no other living thing
  Save that lone fowl and I.

Pale fitful sunshine lit the waste
  That stretched the horizon round,
An ever restless, foaming space,
  By storm-cloud darkly bound,
The deadly Sea, in whose embrace
  Three hundred men were drowned.

The whirling surges, from my grasp
  Oft wrenched the coop away,
But swimming strong I caught again
  My frail supporting stay,
Wherein the bird but feebly stirred
  Half drowned with drenching spray.

The gale was broken, and the waves
  Rolled past in bated power;
Dark heaving now, wide vales between,
  Now white in rainbow shower:
How hard for life 'mid the watery strife,
  I fought in that dread hour:

Now battling with the lofty surge,
  Now in the troughy bed,
Now diving through the breaking seas
  That roared above my head,
Now breathless on my back, as one
  In mortal combat sped.

While thus I fought for very life
  The mainmast drifted past,
Like a huge pine tree to the waves
  From some far headland cast.
I clomb the shrouds that hung adown
  And strode across the mast;

But I did not leave my comrade Fowl
  To die—I noosed a rope,
With practised hand I cast and caught
  His cage within the loop,
The while the bird with glittering eye
  Did watch me from the coop;

His prison door I opened wide,
  I set the captive free;
With outstretched neck and fluttering wings
  He joined me from the sea,
In sooth that bird's companionship
  Was everything to me.

PART IV.

Through mists that hugged the parting storm,
  The Sun rolled down the West,
And in the Eastern board the Moon
  Uprose from Ocean's breast.
'Twas calm—the spent, remorseful winds
  Had sobbed themselves to rest.

The drowsy sound of waters round
  Like opiate after pain,
Lulled to vacant quietude
  The whirl within my brain,
While on my head the salt sea spray
  Fell soft as summer rain;

And if I raised a lid, the Stars
  Seemed moving in the sky—
The rising Moon moved to and fro
  Her soft magnetic eye—
My senses wandered, and I thought
  How good it was to die.

Like Child upon a Mother's breast
  I lay upon the mast,
And gently swaying with the waves
  I fell asleep at last,
A sleep so blank, it had no dream
  Of present, or of past;

How long I slept 'tis vain to say,
  When all things were forgot;
The hideous phantoms in my brain
  Died out, I saw them not;
The ghastly crew, the sinking Ship,
  Became an empty blot.

I slept, how long I know not I—
    A waking tremor swept
Across the slackened shrouds of life
    And stirred them as I slept;
I dreamed I heard a Child's glad voice
    And wistfully I wept—

Half conscious that my dream was vain—
    That no such thing could be.
A second cry—it shook my sleep,
    It sounded from the Sea,
I started,—in my dream I thought
    The voice was calling me.

With sudden heat my pulses beat,
    I woke in glad surprise,
I glanced around in eager haste,
    Benumbed, I strove to rise,
But nothing save the hopeless Sea
    Was present to mine eyes.

Stretched on the lonely mast was I,
  Beside me was the Bird,
He clapped his wings and loudly crew,
  'Twas his clear voice I heard,
The voice, that long ago warned him
  Who thrice denied his Lord.

That cry of warning to the night,
  That sharp upbraiding tone,
Now touched me in my desert plight
  When hope a'most was gone;
It told of Him, by man denied,
  Who died for man alone.

My soul was roused—though all untaught
  I tried my best to pray;
I gazed aloft, and half forgot
  The bed whereon I lay;
I saw the Stars—I felt no fear,
  So hushed, so calm were they;

I saw the Moon, and on the Sea
  Her soft reflected light,
A silver-frosted path to Heaven
  For me too pure and bright:
The shining Moon plunged deep in mist
  And left me to the night.

Then creeping Shadows, dismal Fears,
  About my prison stole,
Again I heard the wrangling waves
  Unceasing in their roll,
And circling Ocean's hopeless chain
  Seemed coiled around my soul;

Nor Moon, nor Star, looked down on me,
  The Sea rolled dark as doom;
My mates beneath the ponderous mast
  Lay weltering in their tomb;
At that dread thought I shut mine eyes,
  I dared not face the gloom.

I called upon His holy name,
  "O Lord, deliver me,
I know, the darkness and the light
  Are both alike to Thee,
O Thou who trod'st the stormy waves,
  O Christ, deliver me;"

The shadow lifted—o'er the main
  A moony radiance swept;
And round about, like living things
  The grey waves foamed and leapt;
The mast gleamed white,—in the blessed light
  I bowed my head and slept;

Calm was my sleep, not dull, nor deep,
  Nor stirred by sudden fears,
But tranquil as a child's sweet sleep
  Whose eyes had closed in tears.—
I woke with strengthened heart to pray,
  To pray to Him who hears.

PART V.

As o'er a billow's slope I rose
  I saw a light afar
That on the dim and distant waves
  Was dancing like a Star;
Then fell a ·sudden shower of rain
  Betwixt me and the Star.

No blustering squall, no angry gloom
  Did vex that shower serene,
A filmy fold all white and cold
  The sky and the sea between;
The red Star shone, grew dim, was gone,
  Lost in the silvery sheen.

The moonbeams o'er the falling rain
  A quivering lustre spread,
Then 'settling in a lunar bow
  O'erarched the uncertain shade;
On the waves below, with fainter glow,
  An answering Iris played;

While the low wind that brought the rain
  Did seem to whisper me
With other voice than the dreary voice
  Of Winds that haunt the Sea,
Whispering soft of mead and croft,
  Of Home beyond the Sea.

My heart made answer to the Winds—
  They mocked me and went by.
The Bird kept watch; my listless eyes
  Were fixed upon the sky,
As on the weary mast I lay
  No other watch had I.

I saw the clouds, like Alpine slopes
   They soared above the rain;
And sudden stars, that trembled, shone,
   Went out, and shone again
Through ghostly Mists, whose unseen feet
   Were on the shadowy main.

The slanting shower waxed faint and thin,
   And the silvery veil more rare,
Till, wondrous strange, it took the shape
   Of sails in the gleamy air:
I gazed until mine eyes grew dim
   For I saw that a Ship was there.

Uncertain, through the shifting mists,
   Like some lone wandering Star
That mocks the gaze with fitful rays
   When clouds and vapours are,
The Vessel loomed—an Ark of Hope
   How nigh—and yet how far.

Then Hope and Fear came fluttering near
 That else had done with me;
Hope, pointing to the distant sail
 And soft illumined sea,
And Fear, unto the shrouded space
 Betwixt the Ship and me.

I saw her signal lights aboard
 The sea-fog glimmering through,
And slowly gliding from the haze
 Distinct her outline grew;
Then shadow fell—a driving mist—
 And all was lost to view.

A sudden rift in the vapory drift,
 And her tapering spars appeared;
As if from blessed Heaven she came
 By pitying Angel steered,
The Ship sailed out into the light,
 The doubting mists were cleared.

I held my breath 'twixt Life and Death,
   And watched her from afar.
Her pennant from the lofty main
   Streamed like a Comet Star;
And I knew by the set of the masts and sails
   That the Ship was a Man-of-War.

With stately motion ever nearing
   On the Frigate came:
Beneath her rushing bows boiled up
   A pale phosphoric flame,
And far astern, till lost in gloom,
   Her broad wake shone the same.

Her lights were dancing on the waves
   In long reflected streams,
Her masts and taper spars stood out
   Streaked with the white moonbeams,
Her sails, like Angel's wings, made bright
   The Deep with their shifting gleams;

My hands outstretched, I strove to call,
  But my voice fell faint and low,
Like to the voice of wailing winds
  That through the rigging blow;
My hope was sliding from my grasp
  When the Cock did suddenly crow.

Loud and clear his clarion note
  Flew straight across the main,
And from the Ship's broad echoing side
  Came softly back again—
Again the Bird, with swelling crest
  Crowed shrill his clarion strain.

Then voices fell upon the waves;
  The Ship's fair course was stayed.
"The cry," said they, "seemed there away
  In yonder rain-cloud's shade,
'Twas as the cry of a crowing cock
  Or owl in forest glade."

D

I saw dark figures crowd the poop,
  I heard the sharp command,
The quarter-boat ran swiftly down
  And help was close at hand,
Then came the welcome dash of oars,
  My heart was nigh unmanned.

They slung me o'er the Ship's dark side,
  They laid me in a cot;
As one amazed, my brain all dazed
  I raved, I knew not what,
Of dismal wrecks, of crowing cocks,
  Of dead men left to rot.

Oh who can tell save he whom Fate
  Hath hurried to the brink
Of that dark Stream whose bitter cup
  All men are born to drink,
Who face to face hath stood with Death
  And never a nerve did shrink,

The sharp revulse from Death to Life,
  The passion of the heart,
When, in His mercy from the grave
  Reprieved we backward start—
"O God, unto my shattered soul
  Thy saving health impart."

After a while my sense returned,
  The mind resumed its sway,
And then my yearning spirit burned
  Alone with God to pray,
So for a space I turned my face
  From the watchful crew away.

Calm came at last, great calm and peace,
  And thanks to God I gave.
I prayed in silence—a rough man
  Just rescued from the grave,
I well may leave the thanks untold
  That unto God I gave.

As when before the glorious Sun
  The storm clouds break away,
And from the giddy deck we mark
  The instant noon of day,
All doubts are o'er, the course we fix—
  And steam and sails obey;

So from my Soul by Death o'ercast,
  Perplexing shadows flew;
E'en as I prayed, His guiding ray
  Brought time and reckoning true;
I rose, and told to those around
  The tale I tell to you.

Ship, Crew, are gone—my comrades brave
  Death gave them to the Deep;
There, in a Seaman's quiet grave
  The lost Three Hundred sleep;
Until all hands are called aloft
  The lost Three Hundred sleep.

And if forlorn I roam the World
   And in no port abide,
My faithful Bird he follows me
   O'er Earth and Ocean wide;
I have no other friend but he,
   Almighty God beside.

THE

DEATH OF MAXIMILIAN.

(JUNE 19TH, 1867.)

MAXIMILIAN.

———◆———

THE tropic stars still brightly shone
  Though night was passing by,
When we heard the clank and measured tread
  Of Horse and Infantry;
Armed shadows thronged the Convent ground
  Ere dawn was in the sky.

With sabre, lance, and bayonet,
  The Juarist men were they
Who formed around the cloistered Pile
  Where Maximilian lay;
With traitor hearts, and hands, they came,
  To take our Chief away.

How fared it with his Majesty
  In that old Convent hall,
The Emperor that France set up,
  And left alone to fall?—
France drooped her flag, she sheathed her sword,
  At the Yankee's braggart call;

But he, of Austria's noble house,
  And every inch a King,
He scorned to wear the feather white
  Plucked from the Eagle's wing;
'Twas Honour, versus prudent France
  And Yankee blustering.

But say, how fared his Majesty,
  This King that France had made ?—
Oh shame !—for forty thousand crowns
  Unto the Foe betrayed,
The felon Lopez sold to Death
  The Monarch, France had made.

Entrapped and caged, in that dark hall
  A captive Prince behold ;
The Warrior Chief, for whom but now
  A Host in arms enrolled ;
The Emperor of Mexico,
  Thus basely bought and sold.

In truth, it was a moving sight,
  The King awaiting doom ;
Tears dimmed our eyes, but his keen gaze
  Did pierce the vaulted room,
As if he saw, what we saw not—
  The Light, beyond the gloom.

Death-doomed as he, brave Mejia
    Stood there with Miramon;
"O King," he said, "'tis good for us
    To die, our duty done;
The volley, and the soldier's grave,
    And thou to lead us on."

We raised in haste a simple Shrine
    Whereat the Three adored;
No solemn miserere their's
    From choral voices poured;
The chamber doors were guarded close
    With carbine and with sword.

We heard the muffled drums without,
    The murmured prayer within,
The Penitents on bended knees
    Their last short shrift begin,
The mortal Priest, with broken voice,
    Absolving each his sin.

The Monarch rose—the taper's light
  Died out in dawning day;
"Good Priest," he said, "this farewell note
  Unto my Wife convey,
She knelt before the Frenchman's throne
  In vain—now come away."

They sought to bind his steadfast eyes,
  But sternly he forbade;
"Too often have I looked on Death
  To fear his face," he said,
"No further bondage—Vamonos
  A la Libertad—

Now open wide the Convent gates
  And let your King go through."
The Convent gates they opened wide,
  Out paced the Brave, the True,
Around him closed the Horse and Foot,
  The Priests walked two and two.

Up the lonely road they marched,
  The City on the right—
The houses whitening in the dawn
  Stood sharp against the night,
Each loftier spire, a fretted fire,
  Glowed with the reddening light;

On they marched with muffled drums
  Up to the fatal mound.*
While the unceasing funeral bell
  Swung out in warning sound
The silent City woke, and crowds
  In haste came gathering round;

And faces white, in hate and fright,
  Peered through the shadow grey,
As forward to the gleamy height
  To mock God's blessed day,
With pennoned lance and bayonet
  The death-march rolled away.

* Cerro de la Campána, a rocky hill about one mile from Querétaro.

The Stars slunk down behind the hills—
　The Sun rushed up the sky—
His living rays inflamed with gold
　Death's bristling pageantry,
That men might see in Day's broad light
　Our Maximilian die.

On they marched to the muffled drum
　And ever wailing fife;
Behind him, in the shadow lay,
　A Throne, and earthly strife;
From night, he marched through sunshine,
　On to Eternal Life.

A sharp command—a sudden "Halt"—
　But never a word said he,
The Coffin, and the Squad, were near,
　And ready musketry;
He saw them not, his thoughts were far
　With Her beyond the sea;

He took her portrait from his breast,
  "One kiss before I die."
His back toward the faithless West,
  He watched the Eastern sky;
He sighed, and murmured, "Happy rest"—
  We knew the reason why.

O Lady, from the Fatherland,
  True Wife of Prince as true,
Proud Northern, with the lustrous eyes
  And hair of raven hue,
Princess—Queen—God pitied thee
  And dulled thy mortal view.

Thou knowest not, and may'st not know,
  The toil, the strife, the pain,
The friendships false, the obloquy,
  Of that brief troubled reign;
Beyond the happy rest, O Queen,
  Thou'lt find thy Love again.

The sudden click of the rifle locks
  Recalled his wandering thought—
He proudly raised himself erect
  To die as Monarch ought;
But still one other word had he
  For those who pardon sought;

"O Friends," he said, "and you my Foes,
  How freely I forgive
The gracious God above me knows,
  Who doth my sins forgive;
I fought for Order, Peace, and Law—
  I lost—nor care to live."

A pause—a sudden sharp report—
  The smoke obscured the sky,
A murky veil that shrouded all
  From every staring eye—
The shadow lifted, and we saw
  A deeper Shadow lie.

E

The bullets pierced his manly breast
   As he stood facing Death—
Forgiveness was his dying word,
   Carlotta on his breath.
Be world-wide shame on Mexico,
   Who shot her King to death.

TRAFALGAR.

WRITTEN IN 1865,

IN COMMEMORATION OF THE CENTENARY.

OF THE

FLAG-SHIP "VICTORY."

TRAFALGAR.

Oh, listen to my story, boys,
　Of sixty years agone,
Of England's naval glory, boys,
　A battle fought and won;
How Nelson died off Trafalgar,
　October twenty-one,

'Twas in the flag-ship, Victory,
  We sailed from Portsmouth Dock,
To chase the Fleets of France and Spain,
  And bring them to the block;
So we cruised about for a week or two
  Off Gibraltar Rock.

On Sunday, sighting Trafalgar,
  We shortened sail at night,
Till, in the grey, where a Frigate lay,
  We saw, by the dawning light,
Her signal flying,—"East by South,
  The Enemy in sight."

Lord Nelson he stood on the quarterdeck,
  In the old fighting coat was he,
His stockings were silk, and as white as milk,
  His breeches to the knee,
As he stood looking out with eight hundred men
  From aboard of the Victory.

His Lordship he spied with his glass to port,
  And he spied o'er the starboard bow,
And he saw the Foe, in the flush of the morn,
  A-sailing all of a row;
Says he, as he shut his spying-glass,
  " My Lads we have got 'em now "!

" Up helm—square yards—set every rag
    Of canvas that can draw,
Stunsails alow and aloft!" said he,
  As soon as the Foe he saw;
And the fleet bore up at break of day,
  Off the shoals of Trafalgar.

Lord Nelson led the weather line,
  Lord Collingwood the lee;
The sun, red shining on the sails,
  'Twould do you good to see,
As down we steered in a double row
  To meet the Enemy.

The rolling drums from ship to ship
  The beat to quarters gave,
Then all was hushed, not a sound was heard
  Except the splash of the wave,
As we slipped through the water, to blood and slaughter,
  And to die the death of the brave.

Lord Nelson he stood on the lofty poop
  Of his flag-ship Victory;
He stood looking out, as if he saw
  A sail none else could see;
"Run up aloft one signal more,
  A message from Home," said he,

"ENGLAND EXPECTS THAT EVERY MAN WILL DO HIS DUTY."

Then rolled adown the well manned Fleet,
  Our English battle cry,
A Cheer, the startled Foe could hear
  As he lay waiting by,
An answering cheer, that spoke out clear,
  We conquer or we die;

It ceased—At noon with sudden roar
The slumbering cannon woke,
Quick jets of flame leaped nimbly forth
From the ribs of the bellowing oak,
And heaving through with blazing sides
The Enemy's line we broke.

Our guns laid low four hundred men
As we raked the Bucentaure;
Redoubtable, she lay ahead,
And the Neptune 84,
But we rolled along, and we took their shot,
And the shot of as many more.

And soon came ranging up astern
The fighting Temeraire,
And many a fine old ship whose name
The rolls of History bear,
With English hearts and hands they came,
And cheers that shook the air.

Our hull was wrapped in sulphurous clouds,
  Though aloft the sky was bright,
And the fluttering flags streamed proudly forth,
  And the sails gleamed snowy white,
While the work of death went on beneath,
  In the noisome smoke of the fight.

Tier on tier of low laid guns
  Incessant broadsides poured,
O'er the red waves the glancing shot
  Dashed through the foam, aboard,
And far and wide, as one huge voice,
  Continuous thunder roared.

The flag for closer battle flying
  We nailed it to the mast—
As 'twixt the Enemy's blazing lines
  The vengeful Victory passed,
With broadsides right and left replying
  We brought them to at last.

Yard to yard, muzzle to muzzle,
　The grappling Squadrons· close;
Blinding dust, hot stifling smoke
　From the fiery shambles rose;
We scarce could tell, in that seething hell,
　Our Comrades, from our Foes.

At 1.15, Lord Nelson fell,
　And forty men around him;
A ball from the Redoubtable
　Most grievously did wound him;
At half-past four o'clock he died,
　And Glory came and crowned him.

The setting sun through angry gloom
　Reddened our sails again;
The fight was done, the victory won,
　And the Fleets of France and Spain
Their flags hauled down, like worthless logs
　Lay strown about the main.

We swabbed up the decks, we straightened the dead,
  We numbered that ghastly crowd,
We sunk them with shot in their deep sea bed
  While winds were piping loud;
With a seaman's prayer, we left them there,
  Each man in his hammock shroud.

Nelson, we kept for an English grave,
  We hove not his corse to the sea;
We held it in trust for mother Earth
  Till the day of his burial be,
In the coffin brave, Ben Hallowell gave,
  From the Orient's mainmast tree.*

We plugged up the Victory's shattered sides
  Riddled with cannon balls—
We weathered the shoals off Trafalgar,
  Nor cared for the blustering squalls—
We dashed through the foam to our Island Home,
  And we gave the Great Dead to St. Paul's.

A hundred years old is the Victory,
  And with all our hearts we love her;
The glory of her Nelson's death
  Is ever around and above her,
As she lies on her guard, off Portsmouth Hard,
  Though her fighting days are over.

Then cheer, boys, cheer for the Victory,
  The brave Flag-ship of yore,
Of Her, the memory shall not die
  Till Time itself be o'er;
To Nelson—he is gone aloft—
  Silence—and nothing more.

NOTE.

* " After the battle of the Nile, 1798, part of the mainmast of the French Admiral's Ship l'Orient was picked up by the Swift-sure. Captain Hallowell ordered his carpenter to make a coffin of it; the iron as well as wood was taken from the wreck of the same ship: it was finished as well and handsomely as the workman's skill and materials would permit; and Hallowell then sent it to the Admiral with the following letter:—' Sir, I have taken the liberty of presenting you a coffin made from the mainmast of l'Orient, that when you have finished your military career in this world you may be buried in one of your trophies. But that that period may be far distant, is the earnest wish of your sincere friend Benjamin Hallowell.' An offering so strange, and yet so suited to the occasion, was received by Nelson in the spirit with which it was sent. As if he felt it good for him, now that he was at the summit of his wishes, to have death before his eyes, he ordered the coffin to be placed upright in his cabin. Such a piece of furniture, however, was more suitable to his own feelings than to those of his guests and attendants; and an old favorite servant entreated him so earnestly to let it be removed, that at length he consented to have the coffin carried below: but he gave strict orders that it should be safely stowed, and reserved for the purpose for which its brave and worthy donor had designed it."— Southey's *Life of Nelson.*

I. E. Chillcott, Steam Press, Clare Street & St. Stephen's Avenue, Bristol.